D0877479

the failure six

shane jones
the failure six

fugue state press

new york

Library of Congress Control Number 2009928957

ISBN 978-1-879193-19-2

Front cover illustrations by Zach Dodson
Text illustrations by Chris Pell

Excerpts of this book first appeared in
New York Tyrant and *Lamination Colony*

Published by Fugue State Press
PO Box 80, Cooper Station
New York NY 10276

www.fuguestatepress.com
info@fuguestatepress.com

For my brother, Blake.

the failure six

1. Antun

2. Bilo

3. Cecile

4. Ernest

5. Philip

6. Foe

ANTUN

The first failure, Antun

The messenger was given an address by way of pushed note under his door.

The messenger had been dreaming of owls and capes. In his dream he saw a revolver go off inside the owl's cape. The revolver made a coughing sound and the wounded owl opened his mouth and made a sound like paper being pushed across a floor.

The messenger woke, blew out the candle on his nightstand, and saw a white pamphlet inside a large sheet of brown paper on the floor.

The person outside the door had a dream the night before too. It was of rainbow colored blobs falling from a pea-green sky.

Antun was the messenger's name. Two pastel blue-colored triangles were stuck on his face.

The message read Enclosed pamphlet, please find necessary information to relay to seamstress.

#

The address brought Antun to 115 Porter.

Antun knocked on the wooden front door. He wore a cape and felt foolish for doing so.

He knocked again.

He retied his cape.

He read from the pamphlet It is imperative that you enter the household even if the seamstress refuses to answer.

Antun had never had a message assignment like this. He had been a messenger, and quite successful if you asked anyone in the town, for three years.

Most messages were small scraps of parchment handed over to housewives. Sometimes the housewives would break down in tears. Sometimes the housewives would form fists.

Once, a young girl threw the message back at him.

She opened her mouth and formed a square wave of sound that filled the room.

\#

Antun opened the door.

He walked into a room dimly lit by green glass lanterns. Three cats sat upright in rocking chairs smoking pipes. Their faces were spinning wheels of color, puffs of white smoke billowing from the center. Many papers covered a properly polished black floor.

Sitting in the center of the room, a girl wearing a brown dress, velvet-laced, in blood.

\#

Antun struck a match and read from the pamphlet.

His hands trembled.

He felt the air, with its swirling scents of turpentine, beeswax, and smoke, being sucked from his throat.

One of the cats began playing a guitar. Another opened a book by Lewis Carroll and the spinning face of color sighed, causing a large cloud of white smoke to puff out and float up to the ceiling.

Antun thought about the dignity that owls possess.

He lit another match and read the first section of the pamphlet before the tiny flame went out. In his mind what he read aloud sounded like:

> Your name is Foe. You are a seamstress who earns a decent living through your ways with linen and silk. Your mother died in an automobile accident in the countryside when you were twelve and your father lost a duel to

a man with a green mustache. Your father
was drunk during this duel. He would have
won. You cried a lot. There was no one to
comfort you so you began your lonely appren-
ticeship in sewing.

The girl didn't move. Her head was cocked to the
side and for a moment Antun thought she was dead.
Then she yawned and wiped some blood from her
exposed legs and onto some papers.

#
Partial List for Messengers

Do only as instructed by given cover note.
Emotional interaction with recipient is frowned upon.
Once message is delivered leave the household.
Appear stoic.
Dress appropriately for the delivering of bad news.
Almost all messages will be passed by written note.
In rare cases, the messenger will be required to become orator.
The hunting of animals is encouraged.
A messenger must possess an excellent memory.
Payment will come in the form of gold doubloons placed upon your pillow.

#

An honest mistake, Antun had read the second page of the pamphlet instead of the first. He felt a terrible guilt and in the process of striking another match nearly lit the entire pamphlet aflame.

He straightened the triangles on his face. One was upside down against the other.

Without a doubt, he thought, he would be stripped of his title as messenger when he got back to his room.

He imagined it now, the black note flicked under his door followed by a dream cough to wake him. It will happen later tonight, Antun thought.

> Your name is Foe, Antun heard in his mind.
> Your last name is Lovell. You were born in
> the country but your parents moved to the city
> when your father took a position as a steel
> worker. You're twenty years old.

The girl stood up. She walked over to a table where a violin was. She picked up the violin and started playing along with the guitar-playing cat. They performed a little song together, nodding their heads and stomping their feet.

After a minute, they stopped.

> Why are you wearing a cape, the girl wrote on a sheet of paper.

Antun struck another match. The girl brought over a lamp and held it near Antun's face so they could read what they were saying.

> My name is Foe.

> Yes, wrote Antun.

> My parents are dead.

> I'm afraid so.

> Can you tell me why.

Antun re-read the section on how her mother and father had passed. The girl sat back down on the

floor. The blood was gone. The cats were outside
silently meowing. There were clouds on the ceiling
and there were little black crosses bobbing up and
down in the clouds.

But who are you, the girl wrote.

I'm a messenger.

What's my name.

Foe.

Oh good, the girl wrote.

Foe walked to a long table at the far side of the room.
Antun could only see a vague outline of her dress.
Then he saw a candlestick angled in mid-air.

When Foe came back across the room she handed
him a small square of brown paper with a wax seal,
the initials DH pressed. In smaller writing, at the very
bottom, The Nightmare Papers.

Upon returning to his room, Antun opened the

message and read Please tell my parents to come and take me home. Then he stopped himself from reading any more.

For the remainder of the night Antun waited for the black note to be pushed under his door but it never came.

\#

Antun fell asleep.

He dreamed the sea eating caped owls. He saw Foe
in a rowboat fishing for dead owls but only capturing
wet capes. On the shore he saw a man with a green
mustache and two revolvers firing bullets into the
chest of an old man.

Antun saw himself feeding city pigeons. A long piece
of string spiraled from his pointer finger to the
horizon. Along the string were sea-wet pieces of bread
for the pigeons.

\#

The next morning Antun purchased a paper and sat in the park.

Pigeons gathered. It was a sunny day that lit gardens orange. After reading a brief article on political upheaval, Antun scanned the second page and read:

MISSING – WOMAN – TWENTY YEARS OF AGE – BROWN HAIR – WANTED – QUES-TIONING – STATE – CONTACT – REWARD OFFERED – NAME – FOE

And just below:

A MESSENGER WAS FOUND DEAD LATE LAST NIGHT IN SUPTINE ALLEY OF AN APPARENT SUICIDE. POLICE SEEK AN-SWERS. YOU KNOW ANYTHING, YOU TELL EVERYTHING.

A man in a long black coat with large square buttons approached Antun. He wore a dusty top-hat and a scarf covered his face. He dropped a note on Antun's lap and then ran away as fast as Antun had ever seen a man run, into the gardens, tripping several times, clawing at the mud, still running into the distant park fields.

Antun stared at the square of paper. Written on the top it said Return to your room to discover a new pamphlet. Also, a suitable lantern to take with you to 115 Porter.

\#

A pamphlet and a lantern inside Antun's room.

The smell of cider and woodcarvers from the street.

Tree branches reaching through an open window for a cup of tea.

Clipped to the pamphlet was a note that said Bringing pamphlets to 115 Porter is very troubling. We should have thought of this earlier. Please memorize and relay to desired recipient.

\#

Antun arrived at 115 Porter.

The cats were gone. There were four empty rocking chairs.

The girl was stacking books in dozens of tall columns that touched the ceiling.

Hello Foe, how are you.

Antun tried to retrieve the words from the pamphlet but couldn't find them.

Are you okay.

Foe stacked more books. Some of the columns tittered back and forth. Foe snaked her way through the many columns and nearly knocked one over. At the top of one of the book columns was a little cat with a little guitar and his face was a wheel of spinning colors. He waved at Antun. Antun waved back.

Antun saw a man walking down the hallway leading to

the kitchen. The man ducked into a side room.
Perhaps Foe's bedroom, thought Antun.

Don't mind him, wrote Foe. He's just a
Russian candle maker.

Your name is Foe. Your parents are dead.
Your mother died in a car accident and your
father lost a duel. You are a seamstress.

I can't remember anything, wrote Foe. My
memory is an empty well with a bottom that
stretches through the earth. I had a dream
and in the dream I saw my parents murdered
by a man named deliverer. He had a green
mustache. The revolvers he had were the
most expensive revolvers in the world.

Deliverer.

Yes, that was his name. He wore a blazer of
sorts with a badge on the breast that said DH.
He killed both of them by way of revolvers.
There was a beach. Maybe the sea.

Antun pulled the words from pamphlet to mind and from mouth.

> Your mother died in an automobile accident. Your father agreed to the duel which he subsequently lost.

He felt the words were lies. He felt the words make a square wave of sound that sounded like *bhhhhhhhhh-mmmmmmmmmmmmmmmmmmmmmmmmmmmmmmmm-mmmmmm.*

> I want to help you, wrote Antun.

> Help me with what, wrote Foe. Help me with stacking more books in tall beautiful columns perhaps.

> You're bleeding. You don't remember anything. You need a hospital, a doctor.

> Yes, I do, said Foe aloud, which Antun couldn't understand.

\#

Antun ran Foe a bath with owl's breath and two sugar cubes. Her knees were badly scraped and her palms raw. The Russian candle maker stood in the kitchen sipping tea from a small white porcelain cup that had tree branches painted around the edge.

Next to the bathtub there was a short stack of papers that Antun and Foe used to communicate.

What's my name.

Foe.

Thank you, she wrote. You are quite the gentleman.

I think you should go to the hospital.

Why.

For your memory.

Can you just tell me about my life.

That's why I'm here.

Then why aren't you.

Because I think it is a lie, a dream, a nightmare, and a game.

\#

When Antun returned to his room he opened the door and slipped on a black note on the floor.

His bed had been flipped over. It now leaned awkwardly against the wall. His lanterns had been shattered. His wooden dresser tipped over and clothes thrown around as if in a terrible storm.

Lying on his side, he opened the note and read It is of our knowledge and yours as well, being a respected messenger, that under no circumstance should you engage in helping the recipient. Your bathing of Foe is inexcusable. You are now terminated of all duties until further notice. Very shortly, three men with revolvers will be at your door and will escort you to our residence and your waiting suitable punishment. Goodnight.

BILO

The second failure, Bilo

It was shortly before ten in the morning when Bilo woke.

He climbed from bed, noticed the note near the door, ignored it, and went into the kitchen for a glass of milk. It was cloudy outside, yesterday's color faded into gray clouds, the dull brick sides of the city.

He had a terrible headache. It felt like a square wave of sound bouncing around in there.

Bilo didn't turn a light on. He didn't sit down and drink his milk. He stood staring at the note, the possibility of delivering another message.

The cover of the note said 115 Porter to be read here in your room, memorized, and told to desired recipient. Please, no bathing of said recipient.

Later, after a breakfast of eggs, sausage, and toast with jam, Bilo got dressed and tucked the message inside one of his many coat pockets. For in his youth he was a collector of pockets, and still possessed some of the most popular and beautiful pockets around.

He headed out, towards 115 Porter.

\#

Hello. Your name is Foe. Your father died in a duel and he was drunk. It was a drunken duel. Your mother died in a car accident. You're from the country, I believe. That's where your mother crashed her car. She was a nice woman. Your favorite animal is a cat. When you leave your house, and if questioned, you live a pleasant life as a seamstress. Everything is simple and lovely.

The room filled with a square wave. It sounded like *bhhhhhhhhhmmmmmmmmmmmmmmmmmmmmm.*

Foe was sitting in a rocking chair next to two cats whose faces were spinning wheels of color. She was reading a piece of paper. She felt like she didn't know how to sew anything or know her name as her own. The paper she held said If a messenger arrives at your home he is a liar. Don't listen to him. Who knows what they've done to me at this point. I shall be dead. But don't listen to the messengers. Your name is Foe. I have reason to believe your parents were murdered for some undisclosed reason.

Bilo drank from a canteen filled with wine. His coat was open, the white shirt beneath stained purple. He had a square stuck to his stomach that he scratched at. He jingled some coins in his left upper thigh pocket which he referred to as tiger pocket. Then he continued trying to remember the girl's life but couldn't get past the part about her love and dedication to the movement of DH.

Is it true you are a supporter of DH.

My name is Foe.

DH, said Bilo. He's in the papers all the time but I should have suspected you don't read the papers seeing your current state.

Bilo laughed and burped some wine down his chin.

You have no memory. I heard that from a Russian candle maker at the inn on Jacobs. I should give you some of this wine but I won't. I've already had too much. The Russian candle maker said you can't remember.

Bilo slumped against the wall, sliding down to a sitting position, his legs spread wide on the floor of pamphlets. He mumbled some of the words caught in his memory. He told Foe that the State was going to murder women who planned against having children. He slapped himself, vomited a rainbow into his handkerchief, said that she never planned to have children and DH supported her decision with all his heart.

Foe didn't hear a word through the growing *bhhhhhhhhhmmmmmmmmmmmmmmmmmmmmmmmmmm* coming from Bilo's jumping lips.

#

The previous night, traditional in every sense in the world of Bilo, Bilo found himself at the inn on Jacobs.

Due to public drunkenness, he hadn't received a message to deliver in weeks. When the message came to be delivered to Foe, he felt a small sense of pride, duty, but a larger sense of indifference.

At the inn Bilo had made the mistake of insulting a Russian candle maker who earlier in the evening had confided in Bilo that he was responsible for bringing candles to a young woman who lacked a memory.

The Russian candle maker wrote that he lived upstairs from the girl and could hear her screaming *bhhhhhhhhmmmmmmmmmmmmmmmmmmmmmmmm- mmmmm* during the night.

He also told Bilo that the girl was badly cut on the knees and palms and it was a messenger wearing a cape who bathed her.

The insult came when Bilo told the Russian candle maker that the age of the messenger was ruined, over, that no honor remained even since the uprising of DH whom he referred to as a cowardly buffoon.

The Russian candle maker didn't mention that DH was his uncle. Or that he was to report the ongoing happenings inside 115 Porter to him. No, none of that business was written.

\#

Proclamation From DH.

Sent To Police Station.

Section Reprinted In Paper:

WHEREAS, A GREAT STATE IS ONLY AS GREAT AS THOSE INDIVIDUALS WHO PERFORM EXEMPLARY SERVICE ON BEHALF OF THEIR COUNTRY IN ACCORDANCE WITH THEIR IDEALS; AND

WHEREAS, IT IS MY OPINION THAT THE DAYS OF CURRENT RULE ARE MOVING US IN A WRONGFUL DIREC-TION; AND

WHEREAS, THE TERMS HONOR AND RESPECT HAVE LOST ALL MEANING AND IT IS MY RESPONSIBILITY TO RESTORE THESE VIRTUES TO OUR GREAT STATE; AND

WHEREAS, IT IS WITHOUT QUESTION, OR HESITA-TION, THAT MY COLLEAGUES AND I PLAN TO USE FORCE AND HAVE ALREADY DONE SO; AND

WHEREAS, THE APPARENT SUICIDE REPORTED RECENTLY BY THE PAPER WAS OUR DOING AS WAS THE BOMBING OUTSIDE THE STATE BUILDING ON NOVEMBER 19 AND WE TAKE RESPONSIBILITY, AS EVERY INDIVIDUAL SHOULD, FOR ALL OF OUR ACTIONS;

THEREFORE, I ASSURE YOU MORE DEATHS WILL FOLLOW.

#

There was an outside town hall meeting where politicians and people from the village gathered to discuss DH. It was a mild and cloudy day with a strong wind running from the east horizon.

Many stacks of paper were present so everyone could communicate. Some of the stacks were so tall that they touched the sky. They tilted, waved in the air, people grabbed from the middle, but not one stack fell. It was quite marvelous to witness.

The politicians wanted to talk about DH but didn't know anything about him.

DH was seen once in public, by a potato farmer who had come into the city to sell. The potato farmer told police that DH was tall, about six foot four, and thin, like a scarecrow. He wore a long black coat with large buttons running up the front. Also, a dark scarf concealing half his face but it appeared he might have a red beard. His hair was of medium length. He was slipping squares of parchment and pamphlets under doors. When the potato farmer watched too long,

caught the glassy hazel eyes of DH, thought something along the lines of I know who you are, DH
came close and wrote You would be wise to forget
about this little visual hallucination of yours.

Nearing the end of the town hall meeting, a bomb
went off at the far left quarters of the State building.
Two men, a woman, and a horse were badly injured.
A column of papers caught fire at the base and the
flame climbed up and ignited a cloud.

Burnt papers littered the streets. Members of the
State, in their long dignified black jackets with gold-
crested badges, hurried to collect what they could. In
the distance Bilo stood on a grassy hill drinking a
bottle of wine, thinking the members of the State,
hunched over, looked like question marks.

An ambulance bounced wildly down the wrong street.

\#

In a building with hundreds of rooms, a note was pushed across the floor of a small room, under the door, and into a long carpeted hallway. The note was from Antun asking for help. One of the building's many maids swept it up into a silver dustpan and disposed of it.

#

Bilo made another trip to 115 Porter.

Upon his arrival at 115 Porter he was greeted inside by three men in navy colored pea-coats.

Each wore a breast patch with the initials DH.

Each pointed a revolver at Bilo and fired into his chest.

Lying on the floor, he unfolded a message that was contained inside another message which was inside another message and read in tiny letters You have forgotten not only respect, but to respect honor, and for that you shall be punished accordingly.

As he felt the blood soak his shirt, pants, and many pockets, Bilo noticed the Russian candle maker. He was standing behind the three men firing revolvers. His arms were crossed over his chest. His expression was one of anger and revenge and then, was it possible, yes, joy.

CECILE

The third failure, Cecile

All of Cecile's messages were collected at the post office.

She had requested this early in her messenger career and it had been approved and carried on annually.

This morning she walked to the post office, was handed a brown sack of mail, and went back to her room where she made a pot of coffee.

Since the days of DH overseeing the messenger service, Cecile had not turned indifferent like some messengers, but rather she continued to work as if it was her first day on the job.

So when Cecile read of her newest duty to Memorize a pamphlet and recite it to a woman who needs our help to remember her past and move into her future she felt excited as lightning and nearly kicked the sleeping fox at her feet.

#

Bilo woke on a narrow cot in a small room.

A woman in a white mask told him he was in a building with hundreds of rooms. His chest was covered in blood-soaked gauze. When he tilted his head up to look around he saw the walls and floor were covered in fur. He tasted fur in the back of his throat.

> You need your rest, wrote the woman in the white mask.
>
> Where am I.
>
> The past makes little difference to what's ahead.
>
> What's my name. Why am I bleeding.
>
> A message will be provided for you this evening perhaps.

Bilo looked at the ceiling. He saw thick waves of red

fur, white clouds, little black crosses bobbing up and down.

\#

Cecile knocked on the door to 115 Porter.

A young woman of about twenty came to the door.

> Yes. Can I help you, she wrote.

> My name is Cecile and I'm your messenger today, Cecile wrote and handed the paper back.

> Why is your face like that.

The cuts were roughly shaped like a triangle, a square, and a circle, and they were on Cecile's cheek, nose, and just above her left eyebrow. The first was from a knife fight involving the Jillian Sisters Gang, the second from a low-flying hawk while out on picnic, and the last was self-inflicted from the worst nightmare a person is capable of having.

> That's not really important. May I come in and begin my message.

You can if you are quiet. The Russian candle maker is napping. He loves his naps. He is a fantastic napper. Capable of falling asleep in seconds even in the dead of afternoon.

\#

I'm here to tell you about your life. It is of rumored knowledge that two messengers have come before me and were quite unsuccessful. But none of that matters now. I will begin.

No.

Well, I'm going to begin anyways.

I already know my life. You don't have to tell me.

I do have to tell you.

I'm sorry, wrote Foe. I tried to make myself believe I knew my life. I lied.

You shouldn't lie. It's not very honorable.

I know one thing though.

And that is, wrote Cecile.

I have too many nightmares. They are so real they hurt my eyes.

\#

Cecile took her cardigan off and folded it neatly on a desk stacked high with books.

She turned back around and saw the girl in a rocking chair. The girl held a leash that led to a fox smoking a pipe. When the fox nodded his cap fell off and Cecile picked it up and placed it back upon his head. She told Foe that she too had a pet fox. The fox said Thank you to Cecile.

Beginning with how her parents died, and ending with how the girl, named Foe, should try her best to apply these facts to memory in order to leave her house, Cecile relayed the message in perfect form. She felt a small twitch of pride under a rib. It took less than an hour.

She feared that the words would escape the paper, move into a mouth, and come out *Bhhhhhhhhmmm-mmmmmmmmmmmmmmmmmmmmmmmmmmmmmmmmmmmmm.*

My work is done here I imagine, wrote
Cecile.

But why am I here in this room, wrote Foe.
How can I possibly remember everything you
just wrote me when I can't understand it.

I don't have such answers for you. I'm only
the messenger and my job is done now.
Hopefully your nightmares will cease with this
new information. I know they can be quite
awful.

Perhaps, wrote Foe, who was now out of
paper and felt some sadness because of that.

\#

After Cecile left 115 Porter, the Russian candle maker came from the back bedroom and lit the afternoon candles. There were morning candles, afternoon candles, evening candles, and night candles, and they were kept in a large wooden dresser with each drawer containing one type of candle.

Foe was in bed crying. Thrusting her fists under her pillow she felt the sharp corners of paper. When the Russian candle maker walked back out of the room after lighting the last afternoon candle, she unfolded the note.

> If you wake in the night write down your nightmares on this parchment that you can keep safely under your pillow. The messengers are telling you nothing but lies and if you believe them, if their words absorb, many people are going to die.

\#

DH lived in the largest room in the building of many rooms. A team of note takers lived in an adjacent room and another team with typewriters attached to their thighs lived below.

There was also a room full of foxes on leashes. When DH pulled a rope in his room a long trough filled with milk for the foxes.

Next to the fox room lived a man with a green mustache who carried two revolvers. On his door there was a gold plate with the word DELIVERER written.

When DH wanted to send a message he pulled a rope that rang a bell and flashed a light in the note takers room. The team consisted of six note takers, but only three were required to answer the bell. If the rope was pulled with a hard jerk, the bell would ring slightly louder, and lights would flash faster in the room, thus signaling a message of increased importance.

After the message was constructed, the note takers slipped the message under the door where the team of typewriters sat. No doors were to be opened unless given previous permission by DH.

After the message was transcribed onto parchment or pamphlet or plain piece of paper, the message was pushed under the door and into the hallway where a hallway walker, also known in the house as a maid, would gather the message and bring it to the room of the deliverer and slide the message under the door.

Within the next hour, a separate note would arrive under the door instructing the deliverer as to what messenger was to be used.

Between the hours of midnight and early daybreak, the deliverer's door opened.

The deliverer had small feet and wore padded slippers lined with fox fur.

\#

When Foe was ten, she wrote a message to her future self.

It was after three strange men wielding revolvers had threatened her parents in their home. They broke teacups and smashed cupboards and gutted every drawer looking for unsent messages.

Foe wrote to her future self that she would never be a messenger. She wrote she had a terrible memory and her mother stitched her name and address inside all her dresses. She buried the note to herself in the garden in the park and forgot about it when she woke the next morning to her parents screaming.

Bbhhhhhhhhmmmmmmmmmmmmmmmmmmmmmmmmmmmmmm.

#

Cecile found a note while walking through the garden in the park. It appeared someone had fallen down, possibly several times in the mud, and had been running at a high rate of speed. It was near a rust-colored bush, the piece of paper sticking up, just the corner, from the mud.

In town, a silent parade was beginning. Cecile saw police officers looking the crowds over, separating touching arms with their giant blue clubs. What could they be looking for, thought Cecile, and she pulled the mud-covered note from the garden floor.

The note was written in a young girl's writing. It showed a large square. The lines of the square were the letters *bbhhhhhhhhhmmmmmmmmmmmmmmmmm-mmmmmmmmmmmmmmmmmmmmmmmm* and nothing else.

\#

Many summers ago, Cecile received a message from DH. She was being recruited to be a new messenger. At the time, Cecile had little money. She had undergone a long battle with having triangles attached to her face.

The message said to dress appropriately. There was an address. There was mention of being paid handsomely upon acceptance of tasks.

Before she arrived at the written address, while walking, a car pulled up alongside Cecile. An older gentleman with a large beard and pleasant smile said through the rolled-down passenger window that if she wished to continue to her destination she should get in.

When neither of them understood what he was saying he stopped the car and wrote her a message he flicked through the window.

The car was long, box shaped, and well polished. The trunk alone could fit a small elephant, thought Cecile.

The older gentleman, who once she was inside the car, once they were driving a dusty road to a growing building in the distance that was clearly not the address Cecile had memorized on her note, introduced himself as Carl and wished her luck on her test.

> There's a test, wrote Cecile, holding the paper in front of Carl's face for a brief moment as he drove.

> Of course there's a test! This is an important position you know. The acceptance rate is very low.

The building was gigantic. There were a hundred windows or more.

Before speeding off, Carl wrote that the room she was looking for was on the second floor, door 14, labeled with only the initials DH.

Cecile walked up to the building and went inside.

I'm here, wrote Cecile, to a woman wearing a white mask who stood before her.

She must be a nurse, thought Cecile.

Yes, I know you're here, wrote the woman. I can see that you are here because you are standing in front of me.

Yes, that's all true, Cecile wrote back.

You know there's a test. Carl should have told you there is a test.

He did.

It's just that your clothes don't resemble test-taking clothes.

Oh.

You probably don't even know what test-taking clothes look like let alone own any.

I don't.

It's all very well though, wrote the woman, follow me.

In the corner of the room was a desk with a single piece of paper and a pencil. Cecile was instructed that she had three hours to complete the test and upon completion it would be evaluated. Shortly after, she would be told if she had the position.

I'm sorry, wrote Cecile, but all this seems quite strange. What's the job I'm applying for exactly. And how much is compensation.

I apologize, said the woman in the white mask. When her lips moved, the white mask made a crinkling sound like crushed paper. Her words sounded like a muffled *bbhhh-hhhhhmmmmmmmmmmmmmmmmmmmmmm-mmmmmmmmmmmmmmmmm.*
This job is the most important job anyone can ever have and the compensation is a sack of gold doubloons a week for the rest of your life, she wrote.

When Cecile sat down at the desk she was filled with half excitement and half fear. She made sure to sit up straight and act proper. It was warm in the room. A fire was going in the fireplace on the other side of the room. The woman with the white mask sat on a square piece of fur-covered furniture next to the fire. She lit a cigarette. With a small pocket knife, she cut a hole in her mouth and brought the cigarette to her lips.

Flipping the paper over, at the very top of the page, framed by two pictures of horn blowing angels, the words MESSENGER EVALUATION.

Slightly below, a place for name, and slightly below that, a line for place of residence. In the middle of the page there was the following single question:

YOU WANT TO HELP OTHERS NO MATTER WHAT THE CONSQUENCES TO OTHERS:

1) AGREE.

2) DISAGREE.

3) AGREE.

\#

Cecile made three more trips back to 115 Porter and wrote for a combined duration of six hours.

Sometimes she forgot to write and instead made a square wave of sound that extended from her mouth that sounded like *bhhhhhhhhhmmmmmmmmmmmmm-mmmmmmmmmmmmmmmmmmmmmmmmmmmmm.*

But with a great sense of duty and pride, she filled the girl's head with her life.

> Do you feel like you are retaining any of this, your life that is, she wrote.

Foe wore a long dress. She combed her hair with her fingers.

> Yes, she wrote, in a way I do.

> And in a way you don't.

> It's my memory, Foe wrote. It doesn't quite catch words like it should. It's like a well with

no bottom extending through the earth.

The last note Cecile received at the post office informed her that the exercises of reciting Foe's life should strengthen her memory. By this, the third visit, Foe should feel a sense of calm and be ready to enter back into daily life as a seamstress.

> Well, wrote Cecile. What have you remembered. What have you learned of your life.

A stack of papers, written back and forth from Cecile to Foe, had formed a spiral staircase to the ceiling.

> Very little, I fear.

Cecile's heart quickened. Her hands became fists which she fought to unfold. She had never in her employment as a messenger felt such failure.

> But how can that be. Tell me about your parents. No, tell me how you feel about DH and his reaction to the State. Something. Tell me something you've learned. Tell me how your father died.

Foe ran across the room and threw herself on a couch. She stuffed her hands under a pillow where she kept a note on last night's nightmare. The Russian candle maker entered the room holding a miniature fox smoking a pipe in his palm.

Cecile screamed at Foe who had buried herself under a large quilt. Cecile beat the lumps of the quilt with her fists.

The Russian candle maker ran up the spiral staircase made of paper, opened a trapdoor in the ceiling, and threw the miniature fox smoking a pipe inside.

Cecile continued to beat Foe with greater and greater force.

The trapdoor in the ceiling slammed shut. The Russian candle maker ran back down the stairs and extended his arms towards Cecile who once touched upon the shoulders screamed *bhhhhhhhhmmmmmm-mmmmmmmmmmmmmmmmmmmmmmmmmmmmmmmm.*

Last Night's Nightmare Transcribed Shortly After Midnight

I grabbed a rifle from a man standing next to a horse and put it against my throat. The man asked if I was crazy and I said no that I was just having a bad dream. He nodded. I pulled the trigger and my neck tore open. Flowers bloomed from the blood inside my throat. The man made a bouquet and gave it to his wife who sat on the horse. When my body drained of blood I woke up on a white cot inside a large building with many rooms. I left the building and walked through the streets. I noticed a messenger talking to a woman holding a parasol. I asked the woman if I could talk to the messenger in private and she said sure and floated up into the clouds. I asked the messenger if he thought that was odd and he said it wasn't. I asked the messenger if I was having a nightmare and he said I wasn't, that if he shot me right now I would die. I told him that to get out of nightmares I have to shoot myself and he said that he already knew that. He said everyone had to do that. Then he excused himself, put a pistol in his mouth, and pulled the trigger. His body crumpled at my feet. Smoke rose from the back of his head. A fox soaked in milk ran up and dragged the body away. I can't remember anything but I will remember this.#

The last thing Cecile remembered was beating Foe through a quilt stitched with flowers.

Cecile remembered Foe's body curled up in a ball, and how by just moving her fists slightly an inch or two she would be hitting either a shoulder, hip, or foot.

Then, the waxy hands of the Russian candle maker from behind. And now, waking up in a small room with only a desk containing paper and a pencil, a narrow bed with one cream-colored sheet, and a long rope hanging from the ceiling which she reached up and pulled.

A moment later, a note was slipped under her door. Cecile picked up the note. It was a thin piece of small paper with the word Yes written in fresh ink.

At the desk Cecile wrote Please inform me of my location.

She then walked back to the door and pushed the note under. When she looked under the door she saw small feet in shoes like what ballerinas wear and tufts of red fur near the ankles.

Then the feet shuffled away.

A few minutes passed before another note was sent back under the door. This note said There are three of you here now and others will be saved and others will be hurt. We will teach people great lessons here. Please go to sleep now.

ERNEST

The fourth failure, Ernest

Ernest was at the village teahouse.

He had just completed his first message to a girl named Foe. The experience had shaken him. A Russian candle maker had stood next to him, mere inches away, and held a fox on a leash that drank milk from a porcelain bowl painted with ducks.

After his two hours of speaking she seemed to remember nothing. But why would she. Speaking usually sounded like *bhhhhhhhhhmmmmmmmmm-mmmmmmmmmmmmmm.*

His throat was sore. The Russian candle maker advised any type of tea with a generous amount of honey. Ernest felt insulted. His task wasn't complete and like a child unable to properly hang wet clothes to dry, he was led away to another location.

The teahouse was tall and narrow, consisting of nineteen floors. The furniture was all wood, made by a carpenter who was a well-known acquaintance of the owner. Each floor had different-colored wallpaper. And on each wall hung large paintings of country barns. All the wooden beams in the teahouse were covered in odd patches of red fur.

Ernest took his cup of tea to the top floor. You could see the entire village from here. He drank his tea quickly, burning the row of pink squares on his tongue.

What is wrong with this girl, he thought. I have never in my life delivered a message quite like that one. A sense of dread turned him cold. He went back downstairs for more hot water and a good-sized lemon.

Back upstairs Ernest noticed a man sitting at his table. The man wore a navy shirt, tie, and vest. Dangling over the vest, a gold chain with a large charm with thick gold letters that spelled out DELIVERER.

The man was smoking. He had a green mustache and wore a black top hat with a single bird feather. Two revolvers with mother-of-pearl handles were on the table. The man crossed his legs in a manly fashion (he appeared to be wearing slippers and had very small feet) and gestured, while exhaling, for Ernest to come and sit.

Do I know you, wrote Ernest.

Bhhhhhhhhmmmmmmm, said the man.

He then wrote on the paper Ernest had just handed him and handed it back to Ernest.

Does it matter, he wrote.

You could be my murderer or you could be a saint offering me never-ending wealth.

Ha! You're paid quite well as it is, wrote the man. You might not accomplish your job with a high level of shall we say, achievement, but you are paid more than adequately. As for me murdering you here, in this teahouse, pure nonsense. If I were to murder you, I would challenge you to a duel out there in the fields. The man nodded out the window. Then you would be surely killed and yes, then I would be labeled a murderer.

With his free hand the man tugged on his chain.

It's a simple job really. I deliver messages too.
Complications only arise when the messages
fail to be effective. The man paused and
drank his tea. For example, the last three
messengers, and now yourself, have proven
extremely frustrating for us. But maybe it's
our fault. But I doubt that. Wouldn't you
doubt that.

I did as instructed, wrote Ernest. I did as I've
been taught. I did as I have since the day at
the building, the test, all of that.

Nonsense.

I did as instructed.

You have two more chances.

She doesn't remember anything sir. She has
no memory. Very odd, indeed, but it proves
more than frustrating for me. The messages

that we are to speak are useless. No one
speaks anymore.

The deliverer laughed, loud. It formed a square wave
of sound. As he opened his mouth wider the square
wave pushed the walls and ceiling of the teahouse out
several feet. Above, another floor, the twentieth, was
quickly added and the carpenter came down a long
wooden ladder into the nineteenth floor and apolo-
gized for the all the noise.

She remembers, the deliverer wrote. We
have discovered what we have come to call
The Nightmare Papers, and believe us, she
remembers just fine.

#

Ernest couldn't sleep.

The triangles on his tongue moved in circles.

He tossed and turned, lit a candle then blew it out
only to strike a match seconds later. He slept in cold,
what some would consider a freezing temperature.
Even during the winter months he kept a window
open.

Silence in the streets. Ernest imagined hearing the
loud colors of a parade to give him something to
smile about. Maybe Irish folk music played in a small
brick-walled inn. What did that sound like, wondered
Ernest.

The deliverer had given him a second message at the
teahouse. The message, a somewhat cumbersome
and thick piece of parchment, instructed him to do
something quite unusual.

Ernest convinced himself in the last waking minutes
before he fell asleep that it would be for the best.

Messages Retrieved By Hallway Walkers

The foxes play games with my hair. I hope you are well Foe – Antun

My pockets are filled with blood again. Nurse!
– Bilo

Bhhhhhhhhmmmmmmmmmmmmmmmmmmmmmm-mmmmmmmmmmmmmmmm – Anonymous

I'm not a violent person. Please release me
– Cecile

We request more milk. – Foxes.

\#

Before leaving for his second trip to 115 Porter Ernest took a cold bath with peppermint and washed his hair with a fine soap he had been saving for such an occasion.

He spent considerable time trimming his moustache. Extra care was given to twisting the ends with a gold colored wax.

He dressed in a three-piece suit, tailored to fit tight against his thin frame.

Yes, there was a quick stop at the barbershop. Inside, his hair was properly trimmed and slicked back. Cologne was applied behind his ears in two separate drops by a short man who smelled of ham.

When Foe opened the door he was holding an arrangement of country wildflowers. He smiled the way a gentleman smiles.

> Where's the Russian candle maker, Ernest wrote, then walked down the hall, looking for

Foe's bedroom.

He isn't here today. He said he would be gone for several hours. Would you like something to drink.

Milk, said Ernest. No, let's have brandy. Or maybe a fine wine circa 1864 if you have it.

They drank a small amount of brandy in her room. From his inside jacket pocket Ernest pulled a small book of English poems which he held to the side so Foe could see. He ran his finger under each line and his mouth moved and made the sound *Bhhhhhhhh-mmmmmmmmmmmmmmmmmm.*

It was when Foe excused herself to the bathroom that Ernest extracted the message from his vest pocket. Attached with carpenters glue to the back of the message, a pill. Ernest peeled the pill off and crushed it between his thumb and finger. Rubbing his thumb and finger together, he sprinkled the powder into Foe's glass and stirred it with a wooden dowel he found on top of her dresser.

The powder, whatever the concoction, took quick effect.

What sort of game of rot have I gotten myself into, Ernest thought.

He remembered the deliverer and the two revolvers on the teahouse table. He imagined his own death. He saw himself looking through the eyes of a police officer who had just found the body of a young man named Ernest crumpled and bloodied in a filthy village alley.

From somewhere in the street, Irish folk music. Or at least Ernest thought so. Impossible. A dream. A nightmare. A failure running through the stitching of all clothing, chimneys, clouds.

He began undressing Foe.

So many buttons for a drab-looking dress!

After taking his clothes off, Ernest guided Foe down on the bed. She mumbled something as he pressed his body against her. Next to her head, he had placed the unfolded message, which he now read from as he moved his body accordingly.

With an outstretched hand, Foe reached for a piece of paper to write her nightmare down. A man was on top of her, making the movements of love making that she had read from a book of poems he had brought for her with country wildflowers.

She saw a man in the nude. Yes, he was in the nude, very handsome, and she was as well, nude. Things were hazy. Fur-covered clouds were on the ceiling with little black crosses bobbing up and down.

Ernest continued reading her life story into her ear.

Bbhhhhhhhhhmmmmmmmmmmmmmmmmmmmmmm-mmmmmmmmmmmmmm.
Bbhhhhhhhhhmmmmmmmmmmmmmmmmmmmmmm-mmmmmmmmmmmmmmmmm.
Bbhhhhhhhhhmmmmmmmmmmmmmmmmmmmmmmm-mmmmmmmmmmmmmmm.
Bbhhhhhhhhhmmmmmmmmmmmmmmmmmmmmmmm-mmmmmmmmmmmmmm.
Bbhhhhhhhhhmmmmmmmmmmmmmmmmmmmmmmmm-

mmmmmmmmmmmmmmm.
Bbhhhhhhhmmmmmmmmmmmmmmmmmmmmmmmm-
mmmmmmmmmmmmmmm.

When Ernest was done, he dressed quickly and left
115 Porter. The Russian candle maker was waiting
outside. When he saw Ernest, he flicked his cigarette
and headed inside with great haste.

#

Forgoing the teahouse, Ernest decided on the inn on Jacobs for a drink.

He had never been to the inn on Jacobs before.

A glass containing alcohol, he thought, that will calm my mind.

At a corner table he drank from a beer stein. A woman approached and introduced herself by way of message as Foe. She wore a black costume mask.

Excuse me, wrote Ernest.

May I sit.

Your name.

Foe.

I'm sorry.

Sir, my name is Foe.

The woman looked identical to the woman at 115 Porter with the exception that she was slightly older perhaps. The mask proved difficult with its lined fur. Ernest stood and pulled a chair out.

Excuse me for being so forward, wrote Ernest.

Impossible in this day and age.

Are you the same Foe who lives at 115 Porter.

Of course I am. Who else would have a name like Foe.

The message I relayed to you said you weren't to leave your home. Does the Russian candle maker know about this.

Yes, she wrote, taking Ernest's glass and sipping from his mug. It's fine. I want to go to the sea. I want to live in a strange house next to the sea even if it erodes from the salt and I drown in the sea.

Ernest looked around the inn. He noticed cats sitting at the bar, cats playing cards, and an old cat trying to kiss a young cat wearing a fox-fur coat. He inspected his own hands, touched his face, and ran the triangles on his tongue across the roof of his mouth.

What's the matter, wrote Foe.

Nothing at all.

The house would be on stilts, right where the water breaks. I know that's impossible, but I would make it happen because I would be a millionaire and tell the architects that cost was no object.

I think I'm having a nightmare, wrote Ernest.

He felt beneath him for the comfort of his own bed.

I imagine we are, said Foe and laughed.
Here, I brought us each a revolver.

Proclamation on how to Escape a Nightmare Printed
in Newspaper Ten Years Prior to Current Events

WHEREAS, A GREAT STATE IS ONLY AS GREAT AS
THOSE INDIVIDUALS WHO PERFORM EXEMPLARY SERVICE
ON BEHALF OF THEIR COUNTRY IN ACCORDANCE WITH
THEIR IDEALS; AND

WHEREAS, IT HAS COME TO THE STATE'S ATTEN-
TION THAT THE WAVE OF NIGHTMARES IS A SERIOUS
EPIDEMIC; AND

WHEREAS, AFTER NUMEROUS MEETINGS WE, THE
STATE, HAVE COME TO THE CONCLUSION THAT IN
ORDER TO ESCAPE A NIGHTMARE PREMATURELY, ONE
MUST TAKE HIS OWN LIFE; AND

WHEREAS, IT IS HIGHLY RECOMMENDED THAT YOU
SLEEP WITH EITHER THE FOLLOWING UNDER YOUR
PILLOW OR ON NEARBY NIGHTSTAND: REVOLVER,
POCKET KNIFE, ROPE; AND

WHEREAS, IN SEVERAL CASES, PERSONS WHO
REMAIN IN NIGHTMARES FOR AN EXTENDED PERIOD OF
TIME WAKE UP PSYCHOLOGICALLY DAMAGED AND IT IS

NOT THE STATE'S RESPONSIBILITY TO TREAT THESE
PEOPLE;

THEREFORE, WE, THE STATE, WHO ARE HERE TO
HELP, OFFER THIS ADVICE FROM OUR SELFLESS HEARTS.

#

Ernest woke.

He was nude. Pulling a linen sheet around himself, he walked to the bathroom where he inspected his face, ears, and neck. He had a nasty scar on his chin that wasn't there before.

What happened to me, he thought. Where is Foe.

He ran water for a bath and added some owl's breath and sugar cubes.

There was a knock at the door. Ernest looked through the peephole of his front door. It was the deliverer. He was loading bullets into one of his revolvers.

> I see you Ernest, wrote the deliverer and slid the note under the door as Ernest walked away. Now please open the door.

Quickly, Ernest dressed and walked to the bathroom where there was a small window he had snuck out before. He had had a dream where he jumped through the window and landed on a parade of balloons.

As Ernest squeezed through the window, the deliverer stepped back, fired two shots into the doorknob, and the door swung open.

Ernest! the deliverer shouted as he circled the first room, then, Ernest! as he ran down the hall, passing the bathroom and into the kitchen where he yelled, Ernest! and then back down the hall and into the bathroom where the cold air from the open bathroom window swirled around his bare ankles.

\#

Ernest sat on a park bench.

He had nowhere to run. He knew he would be caught. He questioned himself as to what he was even running from.

A man called the deliverer carrying two revolvers, that's what he was running from, he wrote to himself.

He watched a silent marching band move through the park.

I am doomed, thought Ernest.

Passing through the park, an older man and woman holding hands laughed at Ernest.

> So dramatic, said the woman.

> Ah, the dark troubled waters of the young, said the man.

The couple was laughing so hard they couldn't stand.

They sat on the muddy grass. Soon, they were lying on their sides, struggling to breathe.

The deliverer approached from the back of Ernest who was yelling at the couple. Ernest didn't know what they were saying but could tell they were laughing. People of speech and hearing, thought Ernest, disgusting.

The deliverer drew his revolver and aimed at the back of Ernest's head. The couple stopped laughing and by way of kicking feet and scurrying backward hands, retreated.

> Yes, it is of no laughing matter! said Ernest. What is wrong with you people. No sense of respect. Hearts black as coal!

His words pushed a square wave of *Bhhhhhhhh-mmmmmmmmmmmmmmmmmmmmmmmmmmmmmmmmmm* through the park and into the horizon where birds scattered into the sun and moon. He felt the warm barrel of the revolver on his neck, then shoulder.

Soon, he would be led to the large building with many

rooms, his right shoulder bloodied and poorly wrapped in gauze.

A woman with a white mask, a small hole for her cigarette, waited on the front steps.

PHILIP

The fifth failure, Philip

Such an unfortunate case.

Three men, hand-selected by DH, were appointed to fetch Philip after he had, for reasons unknown, disregarded his duty as a messenger and engaged in personal conversation with Foe at 115 Porter. By DH, and by DH only, the three men were known as The Sons Three.

The Sons Three were to shoot Philip three times. One man was to fire at his right hand, the second the left foot, and the third a leg of the third man's choosing. Triangles, squares, and circles would be used to conceal the wounds.

These instructions were written out by DH and each man received a copy.

They found Philip in an alley, petting a stray fox. It was the second man who aimed poorly, into Philip's stomach. It wasn't the man's fault however. There was quite the scuffle. The bleeding was immense and the three men struggled to stop the bleeding with handfuls of triangles.

The first man wrote a faux suicide note and left it next to Philip's bloody body, a mound of yellow triangles stacked inside his stomach.

The Sons Three ran back to the large building where they were punished accordingly. DH composed a proclamation to be sent to the press.

FOE

The sixth failure, Foe

Foe wore a black carnival mask that surrounded her eyes and covered part of her nose. DH described the mask by way of message as fox-like.

She sat in her room with the Russian candle maker. Every few minutes, she adjusted her mask.

A message appeared under her door.

It said to Walk outside and find a waiting car. The driver was a man named Carl who had a pleasant smile. The car would bring her to a destination of prior choosing where her message would be handed over to a man waiting at the front door.

What's my name. wrote Foe.

The Russian candle maker seemed on the verge of tears. Your name is Foe, he wrote.

Thank you.

Stuffed under her pillow, dozens of notes she had

taken about her nightmares. Each one transcribed and sent via carrier pigeon to DH by the Russian candle maker.

Outside, she found the car.

Yes, the driver did have a pleasant smile. The Russian candle maker opened the back door to the car and she got in.

Bhhhhhhhhmmmmmmmm, said Carl.

Please write your words, wrote Foe. All I can hear are squares and triangles coming from your mouth.

Good morning, wrote Carl.

The car ride took fifteen minutes. The muted colors of the countryside. She asked Carl where they were going and what her name was. He only smiled in the rearview mirror.

The car's fine interior allowed for a bottle of wine and two glasses to be placed between the two front seats. This feature, along with the leather seats and red ceiling with little red clouds with no black crosses, made Foe believe she was going to a place of great sophistication.

> We appreciate your support of DH, wrote Carl, turning onto a dirt road, a tiny building in the distance.

> Who.

> DH, Carl wrote, the building growing larger with each bump. You know him very well.

> I'm sorry but I think you're magician.

> I'm not a magician. My brother, perhaps you know him, is a magician. His name is David Hass.

> I meant to write mistaken.

> Oh, I see. Very funny.

The car pulled up to the large building with many

windows. A hundred perhaps. There was a grand entrance consisting of a stone staircase, skinny lamps, and a wooden front door.

> *Bhhmmmm*, said Carl. He apologized, then wrote Here we are.

The deliverer opened the front door. This Foe knew from the gold chain around his neck, dangling against his gray vest, the large gold charm that spelled out DELIVERER. He had a green mustache. He was holding what looked like the world's most expensive revolvers.

> What's my name again, wrote Foe, who was standing just outside the car but the car had already disappeared.

She walked inside the house and was shown to her room. She was told by a woman in a white mask there would be a test but Foe couldn't understand a word she said. Who could.